HUNG LIKE A HORSE

STORY AND ILLUSTRATIONS BY BRYAN LAWRENCE

IN THIS TALE YOU'LL REALIZE A VERY

IMPORTANT FACT.

IT DOESN'T MATTER HOW BIG OR SMALL,

HOW LONG OR HOW COMPACT.

THE MOST IMPORTANT THING OF ALL IS

BEING JUST BIG ENOUGH

AND BEING A GENT IS NUMBER ONE

BEFORE YOU SHOULD BE ROUGH.

THERE ONCE WAS A HORSE NAMED DANNY.

HIS SIZE WAS SHORT AND SMALL.

BUT ALL HIS BROTHERS AND ALL HIS FRIENDS

GREW UP GIRTHY AND TALL.

THOUGH DAN WAS A SMALL HORSE

HE'D ALWAYS UPHOLD THE LAW.

WHEN ANYONE WOULD START ACTING UP

HE'D KICK 'EM IN THE JAW.

EVENTUALLY DANNY WAS SHERIFF

AND SOME HOTHEADS CAME TO TOWN.

THEY ALWAYS WORE BLUE SASHES

AND HE'D ALWAYS KNOCK EM DOWN.

THE GANG LEADER, BOB ROBERTS,

WAS GIGANTIC LIKE NO OTHER.

HIS HEAD WAS HUGE AND AFTER A FEUD

HE KILLED DANNYS BROTHER.

BEFORE HIS BROTHER PASSED AWAY

HE PROMISED BOB WOULD HANG.

AND WITH HIS TWO SIX SHOOTER GUNS

HE BROUGHT DOWN BOBS WHOLE GANG.

BOB SNUCK INTO DANNY'S HOUSE

AND STOLE AWAY HIS LADY.

HE KIDNAPPED HER AND SLAPPED HER MOUTH

THAT'S WHEN HE GAVE HER A BABY.

BOB WENT INTO HIDING.

BUT DAN KNEW JUST WHERE HE WAS.

HE KNEW THAT HE SMOKED OPIUM

AND HE LIKED BEING HIGH ON DRUGS.

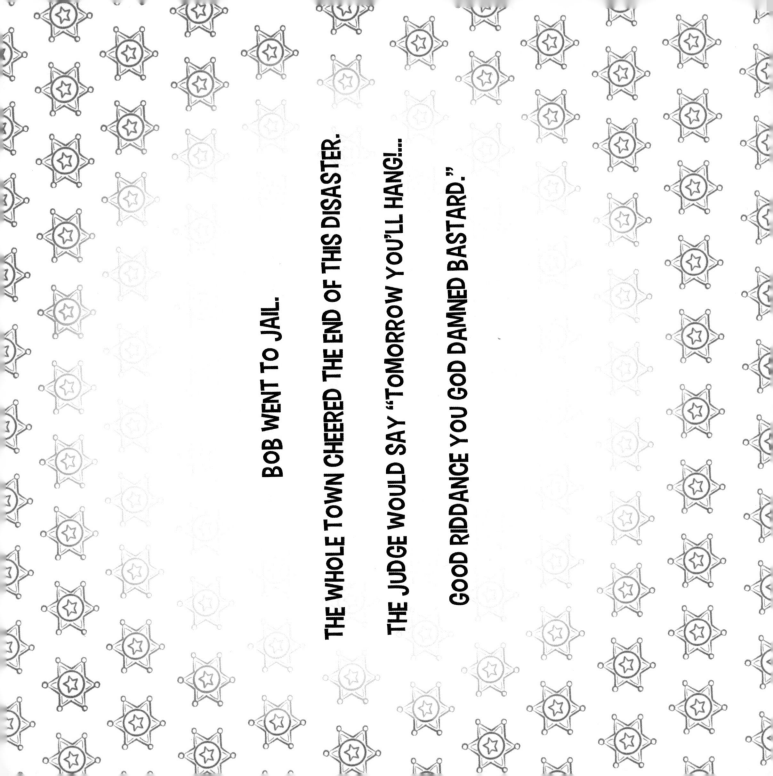

BOB WENT TO JAIL.

THE WHOLE TOWN CHEERED THE END OF THIS DISASTER.

THE JUDGE WOULD SAY "TOMORROW YOU'LL HANG!...

GOOD RIDDANCE YOU GOD DAMNED BASTARD."

YOU WOULDN'T BELIEVE WHAT HAPPENED NEXT

IT'S TRUE! THERE WAS A REPORTER.

"I'M TWICE YOUR SIZE!", BOBS LAST WORDS HE CRIED.

DAN SAID "YOU'RE SIX FEET SHORTER."

THE END

Printed in Great Britain
by Amazon

41497381R00016